Ordinary Mary's Extraordinary Deed

21 20 19   10 9 8 7 6

Published by
Gibbs Smith
P.O. Box 667
Layton, Utah 84041

1.800.835.4993 orders
www.gibbs-smith.com

Edited by Suzanne Gibbs Taylor
Designed and produced by FORTHGEAR, Inc.
Printed and bound in Korea
Gibbs Smith books are printed on either recycled,
100% post-consumer waste, FSC-certified papers
or on paper produced from sustainable PEFC-certified
forest/controlled wood source. Learn more at www.pefc.org.

Library of Congress Control Number: 2017941727

ISBN: 978-1-4236-4887-1 (paperback)

Ordinary Mary's Extraordinary Deed

By Emily Pearson   Illustrations by Fumi Kosaka

GIBBS SMITH
TO ENRICH AND INSPIRE HUMANKIND

Ordinary Mary was so very ordinary that you'd never guess she could change the world. This ordinary kid? She did! She changed the world!

One ordinary day, skipping on her way from her ordinary school to her ordinary house, she passed an ordinary vacant lot filled with ordinary bushes growing ordinary berries—ordinary blue and juicy, luscious lovely berries.

Well, Ordinary Mary picked the ordinary berries and brought them in a big brown bowl to Mrs. Bishop's porch.

What? Left berries in a big brown bowl on Mrs. Bishop's porch?

That sneaky kid! She did!

This made Mrs. Bishop berry, berry happy, so she baked a big batch of blueberry muffins and thought of five people who might have brought those beautiful berries, then secretly gave each a plate.

How great! Five people got a plate.

One of those five was her paperboy, Billy Parker. And when Billy saw his name on a note in the driveway on a plate, he quickly parked his bike and ate every crumb.

Oh, yum, yum, yum, he ate every crumb.

This made him so glad that the next five people got their papers on the porch and not in the bushes where he often threw them. In fact, they were handed right to them!

One of those five was Mr. Mori, who was so amazed that he smiled for ten hours on the airplane, then said to five different people who had heavy bags, "Here, let me help you."

He still smiled, and they did too!

One of those five was Mario, whose cranky little boy James stopped crying when Mr. Mori played peek-a-boo with him until their ride came.

When he waved goodbye, Mario exclaimed,
"How strange that a stranger would be so kind!"

And the next day when he was out shopping,
once, twice, five times he did something nice for
five different people—five times without stopping!

One of those five was Joseph,
old and bent and gray, in front of him
in line at the produce stand.

When he said, "I guess I counted wrong.
I don't really need these oranges,"
little James reached out to him with an
orange from their basket, and Mario
put a coin in Joseph's hand and said,
"Here, take this. The oranges are on us."

As Joseph shuffled to the bus,
his heart was full and his eyes
were wet and his hands did
helpful things for the next
five people he met.

One of those five was Sahar, a college girl who was off to see the world and stopped at Joseph's shop.

When her bag broke and her things fell all over the floor, she said, "Oh, what will I do?"

Joseph said, "This is for you," and he gave her a new bag woven with his own hands in red and purple and green.

"Oh, thank you!" she said, "It's the loveliest bag I've ever seen!"

When Sahar left, she felt sunny as noon, and she just had to shine on five people soon.

One of those five was Sophia, whom she met on a boat, looking like the world might end, looking like someone without a friend.

"What beautiful blue eyes you have," Sahar said, "and they're just the color of the flowers in your lovely dress."

"Yes?" said Sophia.

"Oh, yes!" said Sahar.

The beautiful blue eyes shed a happy tear, and when the boat trip was through, Sophia called five people to make them happy too.

One of those five was Tom, her son the doctor, who was having a very hard day.

"Hi!" she said. "I love you, Tom!"

"Well, how great to hear your voice," he sighed. "I always need my mom!"

Doctor Tom was so cheered up that on his next break he bought a big bunch of bright balloons for five young patients, and he handed them out right then and there.

One of those five was Peter,
a little boy who went home
from the hospital that very day.
Gratitude for the big bunch of
bright balloons filled him and
thrilled him and spilled out of him
and onto the next five people
who came his way.

One of those five was Eric,
a teenage boy whose sacks
and such were way too much.
When one dropped on the
sidewalk, Peter stopped his play
and rushed right over, saying,
"Superwheels to the rescue!"

Well, Eric, no longer stressed,
was very impressed and made
a mental note that very
afternoon to help five
people, and do it soon!

One of those five was Di, his ten-year-old sister who didn't have many friends and was painfully shy.

When Eric said, "Hey, Sis, want to come to the park and learn how to ride my skateboard?" she looked at him wide-eyed.

"Serious?" she cried.

"Sure!" he said.

And because of her brother, Di decided maybe she could be a friend to another five others!

One of those five was Louise, a homeless woman who lived under the trees. She could hardly believe her ears when she heard Di say, "May my brother and I buy you a hot dog and a drink at that stand over there?"

Could it be true? Someone actually cared? Cared enough to give her food and a smiley-faced ring that was practically new?

Louise was so pleased that she decided that even though she had nothing, she would find five others and give them something!

One of those five was Amara, who lost her wallet in the park. Louise found it, full of fives and tens and twenties.

Oh, what she could do with all that money! But she found Amara's name and called her home and over she came.

Amara was so impressed that Louise was honest, when money was something she clearly needed, that she offered her a job in her store, and vowed to do something generous for five people or more!

One of those five was Kate, a woman on vacation who wanted to see a show she'd heard was a sensation.

"Oh, no!" she said. "It's sold out? But I'm going home tomorrow." And her face filled with sorrow.

Amara held out her ticket. "I live here," she said. "I can go anytime—take mine."

Kate loved the show and was so touched that she thought buying five presents for five people back home would really be fun.

And one of those five presents was a little heart necklace for Mary, her niece, and you should have seen her eyes light up in surprise!

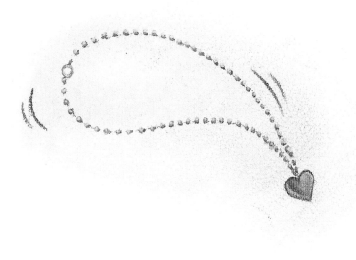

Mary?

What?

Ordinary Mary?

Yes, Ordinary Mary's extraordinary deed had come full circle, and on its way it had changed the lives of every person living!

You see, when Mrs. Bishop made muffins from Mary's blueberries, not only the paperboy, Billy Parker, but the other four people, too, made five people smile, and those five did, too, and after a while—in only sixteen days—love was sent to every person everywhere! Just see how it went:

1

5

25

125

625

3,125

15,625

78,125

390,625

1,953,125

9,765,625

48,828,125

244,140,625

1,220,703,125

6,103,515,625

30,517,578,125

Well, thirty billion is way more than all of the people on the planet, so after everyone had a share and everybody knew that somebody cared, there was even love left over!

The world was changed! And thousands and millions and billions agreed it was all because one ordinary day, Ordinary Mary did a perfectly ordinary, stunningly earthshaking, totally extraordinary deed!